DAY OF THE DEAD

A Celebration of Life

By Polo Orozco • Illustrated by Mirelle Ortega

 A GOLDEN BOOK • NEW YORK

rhcbooks.com

Educators and librarians, for a variety of teaching tools, visit us at RHTeachersLibrarians.com

Library of Congress Control Number: 2023945394

ISBN 978-0-593-70487-5 (trade) — ISBN 978-0-593-70488-2 (ebook)

Printed in the United States of America

10 9 8 7 6 5 4 3 2

It's Day of the Dead! Families gather to remember loved ones who are gone. We celebrate their lives and welcome them back home.

Long ago, indigenous groups in Mexico began to honor the dead. The Mexica believed people went to a resting place called Mictlán after they died. The journey there took four years!

To help loved ones find their way to Mictlán, the Mexica made ofrendas—collections of items such as incense, clothes, flowers, and food that were placed at burial sites as offerings.

In the sixteenth century, Spain invaded Mexico. After that, new and old traditions combined into what is now known as Day of the Dead. In Spanish, we call it Día de Muertos, and it takes place on November 1st and 2nd.

Day of the Dead is a happy holiday. It's when the spirits of our loved ones come to visit the world of the living—and we're excited to have them back! We build altars at home to place our ofrendas on. The altars can be two, three, or even seven steps tall.

Altars look different in every home, but it's tradition to include certain items. At the top of the altar, we put a picture of the person we wish to remember—a grandparent, aunt, uncle, or anyone who's no longer with us. Below that are things our loved ones might use during their visit.

There's a bowl of salt, a glass of water, and incense. The incense cleanses the room and keeps the bad spirits away.

At the bottom of the altar, we draw a cross with ash to help the dead make amends for their mistakes, and a mat called petate is for them to lay on and rest.

But this is a celebration! Toys and musical instruments the dead had owned are also placed on the altar for them to enjoy once again. And their favorite food is served, along with sugarcane and fruit such as plums and pineapples.

Colorful paper decorations
called papel picado are
fun to make.

Cempasúchil—also known as Mexican marigolds—have a bright color and a strong scent. These flowers guide the dead home. Candles also help light their way.

After the ofrenda is ready, some people choose to stay awake and wait for the dead. It's said they come to the altar late at night.

Families open their doors to visitors. Neighbors and friends want to join the fun and remember.

Some families celebrate outside their homes. They decorate and make ofrendas at their loved ones' graves.

With candles everywhere, cemeteries twinkle
on Day of the Dead!

As with any party, food is a must! We offer it to the dead, but the living also get to enjoy a feast. A popular dish is mole, a sauce made with hot peppers and chocolate. It's yummy! We put it on chicken and serve it with rice, tortillas, and a traditional Mexican drink called horchata.

There are sweet treats like pan de muerto. This soft bread is flavored with anise and orange. The top is shaped to look like bones.

Skulls are everywhere during Day of the Dead. Sugar skulls are part of the ofrenda. We also write funny poems to the dead. This type of poem is called a calavera, the Spanish word for skull.

There are Day of the Dead parades. People walk around in snazzy clothes and calavera makeup, all inspired by a Mexican character called La Catrina. She's fancy!

Countries like Peru, Ecuador, and Argentina have their own Day of the Dead celebrations. In Guatemala, festivities include flying giant colorful kites.

In Bolivia, people bake bread called tantawawa in the shape of children and babies.

Latin families all over the world celebrate
Day of the Dead!

The altar is set. Sweet smells from incense and flowers fill the air. Candles light our home. It's time to come together, celebrate, and remember those we love.

¡Feliz Día de Muertos!

A Glossary of Words and Phrases

calavera (ka-la-**beh**-rah): a skull. Also, a funny poem about death.

La Calavera Catrina (la ka-la-**beh**-rah kuh-**tree**-nuh): a character created by Mexican cartoonist José Guadalupe Posada. Her name means "dapper skull."

cempasúchil (sem-pa-**soo**-chil): Mexican marigold.

¡Feliz Día de Muertos! (feh-**lees dee**-ah deh **mwer**-tos): Happy Day of the Dead!

horchata (or-**chaa**-tuh): a sweet, rice-based drink spiced with cinnamon.

Mexica (meh-**hee**-kah): the indigenous people who lived in Mexico during the fourteenth century in the area that is now Mexico City.

Mictlán (**meek**-tuh-laan): "the place of the dead" or the final resting place of people from pre-Hispanic cultures.

mole (**moh**-le): a sauce typically made with chocolate, chiles, and other spices.

ofrendas (oh-**frehn**-das): the offerings made to the dead and traditionally placed on altars.

pan de muerto (pahn deh **mwehr**-toh): "bread of the dead" is a sweet baked good enjoyed during the holiday.

papel picado (**paa**-pel pee-**kaa**-dow): colorful paper with cut-out designs.

petate (peh-**tah**-teh): a woven mat sometimes made of grass.

tantawawa (**tahn**-tuh-wah-wah): a sweet bread often shaped to look like babies and children.